To:

From:

The Broken Ornament

TONY DiTERLIZZI

SIMON & SCHUSTER BOOKS *for* YOUNG READERS

New York London Toronto Sydney New Delhi

Jack wanted this to be the best Christmas ever.

"I want more decorations," he said. "That way Santa will see our house first."

His father chuckled. "Well, you've certainly got that Christmas spirit!"

. . . But it wasn't enough. Something was missing for Jack. "Let's get a BIGGER tree."

"This tree is just fine," replied his mother.

"But Santa needs more room underneath to leave us more presents!" said Jack.

It was Christmas Eve. The house was decorated, the cookies were baked, and the tree had been trimmed—yet Jack still felt like something was missing. He ran into the room holding a dusty old box. "Look! I found more ornaments."

His father sighed. "I think we're finished decorating."

Jack opened the box. A lone ornament lay nestled inside.

"Not that one!" his mother said.

But Jack didn't listen.

The ornament hit the floor, shattering into a million glittery pieces.

"Jack Michael! Look what you've done!"

"It's just a junky old ornament," Jack replied. "We'll get another one."

"No. We can't," his mother said as she went upstairs. Jack's father grabbed a box of tissues and followed her.

Jack knelt down, inspecting the shards. "It was only an accident," he muttered.

In a swirl of shimmering frost a tiny figure formed.

"Are you my fairy godmother?" Jack asked.

A bubbly voice replied, "Godmother? Oh no, they don't trust me with a wand. Call me Tinsel."

"So . . . do you grant wishes?" Jack leaned in close.

"What is it that you wish for?" Tinsel replied. A smile curled in the corner of her mouth like a candy cane.

"I want the best Christmas ever!"

"Then let's deck these halls!" Tinsel tossed a handful of glitter into the air. Each fleck became a fluffy flake of snow. She shook a sprig of mistletoe, and its pearl berries dropped to the floor. From each berry, an enormous Christmas tree burst through the floorboards.

Tinsel tapped her tinkly bells.

The front door flew open. A trio of caroling elves paraded inside, followed by a herd of reindeer, an army of nutcrackers, and a rowdy bunch of snowmen.

"More! More!" Jack cheered.

"Is this merry enough?" Tinsel asked.

Jack's house was the most Christmassy in the whole town . . . probably even the whole world. But somehow something was still missing.

A shiny fragment caught Jack's eye. "Tinsel, can you get Mom a new ornament?"

"No can do," Tinsel replied. "I can give you every ornament in the North Pole, but it won't replace the one you broke."

"Why not?" asked Jack.

Tinsel fluttered near a gingerbread house, and it began to glow from within. "Take a look, Sugar Plum."

Jack peered through the frosting-framed window to see a little girl hanging the ornament he had broken.

"When she was young, your mother's favorite holiday tradition was trimming the tree with her grandma," said Tinsel.

Jack could hear his great-grandmother's voice: "I've had these since I was your age." She handed over the box of ornaments. "Now they are yours."

"That was Great-Grandma's ornament—and I broke it." Jack looked at all the things the fairy had brought. Somehow it was too much and yet not enough. "I wanted this to be the *best* Christmas ever and now it's the *worst*. Can you fix it, Tinsel?"

"There is only one person who can make that kind of Christmas magic," replied Tinsel.

"Santa?" asked Jack.

"No, *you*." Tinsel tweaked his nose. "You silly reindeer."

Like a whoosh of the north wind, an idea rushed into Jack's head. He grabbed pencils, paint, and paper and set off to work.

Jack heard his parents' footsteps on the stairs.

In the blink of an eye, Tinsel's winter wonderland melted away.

"Time for bed, Jack." His mother's voice was soft. "Santa will be here soon."

"Wait. I have something for you," Jack said. "I'm sorry I broke your ornament."

His mother opened her gift. "Aw, Jack, what's this?"

"It's your grandma giving you the ornaments."

Jack's mother looked closely. "But how . . . how did you know?"

"Christmas magic," Jack said with a shrug.

"Oh, Jack, I love it!" His mother hung the ornament at the top of the tree.

Jack's heart felt so big, no amount of wrapping paper could hide it.

Finally, it was the best Christmas ever.

For SOPHIA, *who broke the ornament*

—*Love,*
Papa

WITH SPECIAL THANKS TO *Justin Chanda and the entire S&S team, Steve Berman, Jeanne Birdsall, Holly Black, Lori Holmes-Clark, Grace Desmarais, Scott Fischer, Donato Giancola, William Joyce, Patrick O'Donnell, Jodi Reamer, Emily Rich, Heidi Stemple, Mariah Swanson, Ellen Goldsmith-Vein, David Wiesner, Mo Willems, and Angela DiTerlizzi.*

SIMON & SCHUSTER BOOKS *for* YOUNG READERS
An imprint of Simon & Schuster Children's Publishing Division
1230 Avenue of the Americas, New York, New York 10020
Copyright © 2018 by Tony DiTerlizzi
For information about special discounts for bulk purchases, please contact Simon & Schuster Special Sales at 1-866-506-1949 or business@simonandschuster.com.
The Simon & Schuster Speakers Bureau can bring authors to your live event. For more information or to book an event,
contact the Simon & Schuster Speakers Bureau at 1-866-248-3049 or visit our website at www.simonspeakers.com.
Book design by Greg Stadnyk
The text for this book was set in Century Old Style.
The illustrations for this book were rendered in colored pencil and Acryla gouache on Bristol board. Additional effects were achieved through fairy magic.
Manufactured in China
0718 SCP
First Edition
2 4 6 8 10 9 7 5 3 1
Library of Congress Cataloging-in-Publication Data
Names: DiTerlizzi, Tony, author.
Title: The broken ornament / Tony Diterlizzi.
Description: First edition. | New York : Simon & Schuster Books for Young Readers, [2018] | Summary: In his attempt to make this the best Christmas ever,
Jack accidentally breaks a very old ornament, releasing a tiny fairy who teaches him something about the true Christmas spirit.
| Identifiers: LCCN 2017049085 (print) | LCCN 2017059521 (eBook) | ISBN 9781416939764 (hardcover) | ISBN 9781481479943 (eBook)
Subjects: | CYAC: Christmas tree ornaments—Fiction. | Heirlooms—Fiction. | Family life—Fiction. | Fairies—Fiction. | Christmas—Fiction.
Classification: LCC PZ7.D629 (eBook) | LCC PZ7.D629 Bro 2018 (print) | DDC [E]—dc23
LC record available at https://lccn.loc.gov/2017049085